*Rude
Ramsay
and the
Roaring Radishes*

Margaret Atwood

Rude Ramsay and the Roaring Radishes

Illustrations by Dušan Petričić

KPk
Key Porter Kids

National Library of Canada Cataloguing-in-Publication Data available on request

The publisher gratefully acknowledges the support of the Canada Council for the Arts and the Ontario Arts Council for its publishing program.

We acknowledge the financial support of the Government of Canada through the Book Publishing Industry Development Program (BPIDP) for our publishing activities.

We acknowledge the support of the Government of Ontario through the Ontario Media Development Corporation's Ontario Book Initiative.

This edition is available only for distribution through the school market by Scholastic Canada Ltd.

Key Porter kids is an imprint of
Key Porter Books Limited
Six Adelaide Street East, Tenth Floor
Toronto, Ontario
Canada M5C 1H6

www.keyporter.com

Design: Peter Maher

Printed and bound in Canada

05 06 07 08 09 5 4 3 2 1

For Madelaine and For R. and E. Cook, who will eat almost anything. M.A.

For my curious granddaughter Lara. D.P.

Rude Ramsay resided in a ramshackle rectangular residence with a roof garden, a root cellar, and a revolving door. A rampart ranged down the right-hand side of the run-down real estate.

Residing with Rude Ramsay, who was red-haired, were his revolting relatives, Ron, Rollo, and Ruby. They were rotund but robust, and when not regaling themselves with rum, they relaxed in their recliners, replaying reams of retro rock'n'roll records, relentlessly. This could be rigorous.

While Ron read the racing results, Ruby and Rollo regularly rustled up the repasts. They roasted rice, raisins, rutabagas, and rhinoceros. They rolled out reptiles with a rolling pin. They refrigerated rhubarb and broiled ribs, raviolis, and reindeer rinds on the rotisserie. The rice was rock-hard, the ribs rubbery, the raviolis wrinkled, the rhinoceros raw. The reptiles were still writhing, the rhubarb was runny, and the reindeer rinds were rotten.

Every Friday, Rude Ramsay rebelled. "This repast is repulsive," he'd report. "The rice is riddled with roaches, the raisins are rancid, and the reindeer rinds reek. I feel like regurgitating!"

"Ramsay, you rash, repulsive, red-headed runt! How rude! Rinse your mouth out with rope!" raged Ramsay's revolting relatives, Ron, Rollo, and Ruby. "Repent! Repent!"

"I refuse," retorted Ramsay.

Thoroughly riled, the three revolting relatives rose from the rejected repast and rushed after Ramsay, hurling ratchets, wrenches, wristwatches, rubber boots, and radios, which rebounded off Ramsay's rear. But Ramsay was a rapid runner, and he raced up to the roof garden and down to the root cellar and round and round the revolving door, until his robust but rotund relatives could no longer respire, and required rest.

This ruckus was regarded by numerous racoons, rabbits, robins, rollicking wrens, and rowdy raggedy ravens, who were all roosting on the right-hand rampart, relishing the race and repeating, "Rah! Rah!" raucously.

Ramsay's only friend was Ralph, the red-nosed rat, a
rubicund rodent. While Ramsay reclined upon a rumpled
rucksack near the trash heap, rubbing his rust-coloured bruises,
Ralph rummaged among the roach-riddled rice and the rancid
raisins and the remnants of reeking rhinoceros, remarking,
"Rubbish is ravishing to rats. We revel in rotten reindeer rinds."

"Ripping for you," Ramsay retorted wretchedly. "You are a
rat. But I'm ravenous. All this repeated running round and
around is ruining me. I refer also to the retch-making recipes I
am required to devour, and which I resent. I am less robust than
my revolting relatives. I am receiving a raw deal. It rankles!"

"You might rove to the other side of the rampart," reflected
one of the raggedy ravens. "Relocate your inner realm! Revive
your rapport with nature! Refreshment awaits you there!"

"Be realistic," Ramsay replied. "The rampart is rough. It rises ridiculously high, and it is replete with rocks."

"I remember a round, Roman-vaulted rat-hole," remarked Ralph the red-nosed rat, while grooming his greasy whiskers. "It traverses the rampart, and might be wriggled through."

"Risky," retorted Rude Ramsay. "If rammed in rather far and unable to retreat, I will repine. Then, if it rains, I will drown. Rigor mortis will set in, as well as wrinkles. I am reluctant."

"Rise to the occasion," responded Ralph. "Resist restrictions! Be rugged!"

Together the pair resolved to dare the Roman-vaulted but risky rat-hole, which was crammed with rusty rivets, and assorted remnants, and the remains of rat nests, and was dripping with rivulets from the ragged rents in the rodent-riddled rampart. Ralph rocketed recklessly through, but Ramsay had to crawl, creeping over dark rubble and through narrow turnings, ripping his trousers on sharp rocks, wrecking his rubber-soled runners, and scraping his fingers.
At last a rewarding ray of light pierced the remote end of the rat-hole.

Ramsay emerged into a resplendent realm. A ranch-sized garden with a river rippling through it revealed itself to his regard, rendering Ramsay rhapsodic. A rowboat rocked restfully. Roses enriched the redolent air with their aroma. Raspberry bushes were ranged in reassuring rows.

Ramsay roamed among the raspberry rows, ripping off ripe raspberries and cramming them into his mouth. Ralph rambled restlessly, ransacking the region for root vegetables.

"Radishes! Radishes!" Ralph briskly reported.

"Right you are!" Ramsay responded. For there, around a corner, were rows and rows of round red radishes, ready to be devoured. Surely they were organic! Ramsay hadn't relished a fresh radish ever since he could remember. What a rare treat!

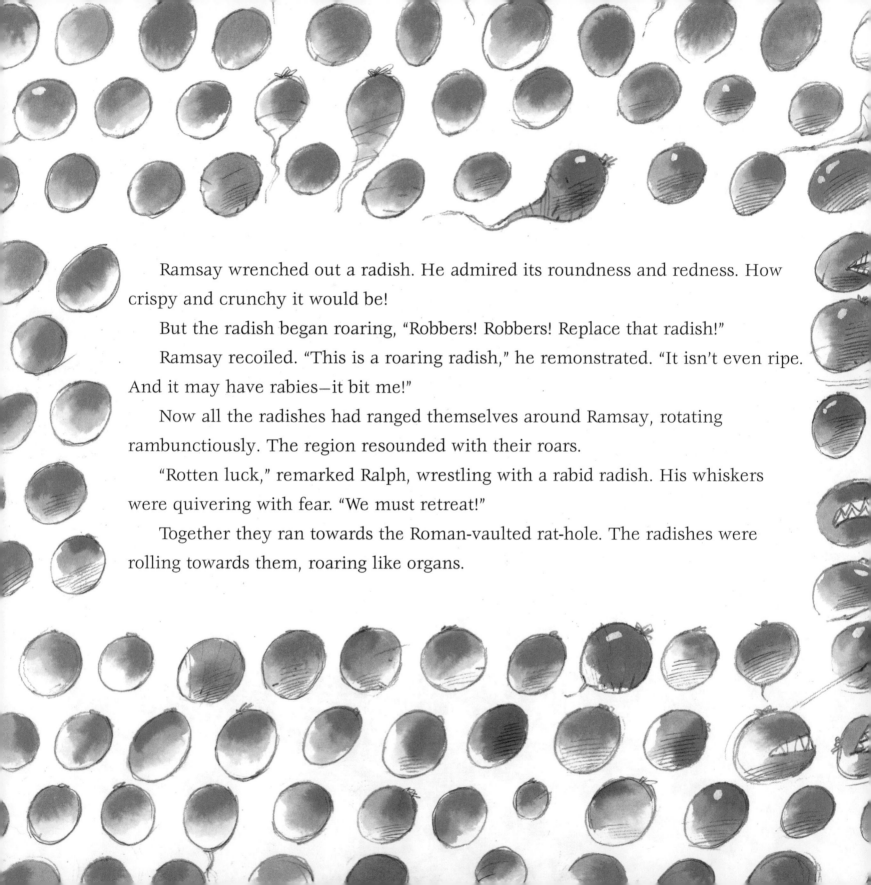

Ramsay wrenched out a radish. He admired its roundness and redness. How crispy and crunchy it would be!

But the radish began roaring, "Robbers! Robbers! Replace that radish!"

Ramsay recoiled. "This is a roaring radish," he remonstrated. "It isn't even ripe. And it may have rabies—it bit me!"

Now all the radishes had ranged themselves around Ramsay, rotating rambunctiously. The region resounded with their roars.

"Rotten luck," remarked Ralph, wrestling with a rabid radish. His whiskers were quivering with fear. "We must retreat!"

Together they ran towards the Roman-vaulted rat-hole. The radishes were rolling towards them, roaring like organs.

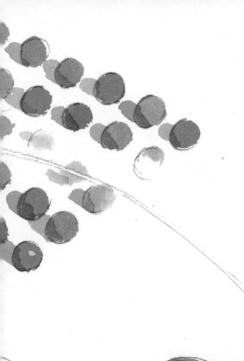

But then a small girl appeared. She had a red ruffled frock, raven ringlets with ribbons, and ribbed legwear. Over her arm she carried a receptacle for roses and raspberries.

"Why are you robbing me of my radishes?" she queried.

"What radishes?" replied Ramsay reticently. The radishes had now stopped roaring, and were resolutely re-rooting themselves in the ravaged radish rows.

"My name is Rillah," the small girl responded. "And you must be Rude Ramsay."

"You recognize me?" Ramsay was surprised.

"Only by remote reputation. I frequently hear your revolting relatives repeating that refrain. 'Rude Ramsay, you rash, repulsive, red-headed runt,' they rant. Would you like a rusk?" And she offered an assortment of rusks from her receptacle.

Ramsay and Ralph each reached for a rusk.

"Where do you reside?" Ralph inquired.

"In that romantic but recently-restored rectory with the rotunda," replied Rillah.

Ramsay regarded the rectory. It was indeed romantic. Rhododendrons wreathed around it, fretwork trellises replete with trailing arbutus adorned it, a radiant rainbow arched above it.

"You must be royally rich,"
Ramsay remarked ruefully,
remembering his own ramshackle
residence. His trousers were ripped
and his rubber-soled runners
were wrecked. He resembled
a ragamuffin. Surely Rillah
would find him repellent.
She would never be his friend.
He wished she were a rat.

"Until recently I was
rolling in rupees, but they have
become rather scarce. My
situation," reflected Rillah, "is
the reverse of yours. You are rude,
but at least you have relatives,
however revolting. I am refined,
but my relatives, although
outwardly respectable and
refulgently attired, are lacking
in rectitude.

They rented a veritable regatta of Rolls Royces, but they fell into arrears on revenues.

When the rent collector arrived they all ran off, some by road, some by rail, revealing no remorse. I have been rejected. No one has rescued me. Also, I am bored." And she released a tear.

"Cheer up," said Ramsay robustly. "Do not repine. Let's explore the rectory!"

Ramsay, Rillah, and Ralph the red-nosed rat rambled all over the recently-restored but romantic rectory. They reviewed the rotunda, which had a wide range of purloined reading materials, and the gallery filled with fraudulent rococo artworks, forged by professionals, and the cellar with racks and racks of rare beverages ruthlessly plundered by Rillah's rascally relatives. At last they reached the rumpus room.

"This is the rumpus room," remarked Rillah regretfully, "but there has never been a rumpus in it. My relatives, though racketeers, were too refined for rumpuses. How I would relish regarding a real rumpus!"

"Your request is my resolve," replied Ramsay with a respectful gesture. "Return with me!"

So Ramsay, Rillah, and Ralph the red-nosed rat wriggled back through the Roman-vaulted rat-hole and reached the rectangular residence, where Ramsay's revolting relatives, Ron, Rollo, and Ruby, replete with rum, were relaxing in their recliners to the resounding rhythms of rock'n'roll.

"Ready?" inquired Ramsay.

Rillah grinned in a refined but riotous manner.

"Rotten reindeer rinds reek, and so do Ron, Rollo, and Ruby!" Ramsay blared. "And your rock 'n roll records are ridiculous!"

"Ramsay, you rabble-rouser! You are outrageous!" Ron, Rollo, and Ruby rose from their recliners like red-eyed rattlesnakes and went on the rampage. What a ruckus! Ramsay raced up to the roof garden, reversed direction, reeled through the root cellar, then round and round the revolving door, while his revolting relatives hurled ratchets, wrenches, wristwatches, radios, and rubber boots at his rear. But this time Ramsay ran so rapidly that they missed.

At last the revolting relatives ran out of steam, and relapsed into a recumbent posture.

"Oh, Ramsay! That was a real rumpus!" trilled Rillah. "You may be rude, but you can run with a rapidity that erases boredom!"

"I would be less rude if I resided in the romantic rectory, surrounded by rhododendrons," replied Ramsay, "and could eat raspberries and rusks, instead of raw rhinoceros and rancid raisins."

"True," Rillah responded. "And I would be less tearful. To acquire a friend is refreshing, as well as reassuring."

"Do you like rats?" Ramsay queried, for it had occurred to him that the arrival of a new friend might cause Ralph to feel repudiated.

"There are few creatures I adore more than a rubicund, red-nosed rodent," Rillah replied, stroking Ralph's fur with terms of endearment. "Also, he will crunch up any roaches that may stray from the run-down side of the rampart."

"What about the rabid roaring radishes?" inquired Ramsay. "They regard me as a robber and will relentlessly rend me to shreds."

"They are not real radishes," replied Rillah. "They are robot replicas, cleverly arranged to repel intruders. I will reprogram them so they will be neutral in regard to you."

So, while the racoons, rabbits, robins, wrens, and raggedy ravens all roosting on the rampart cheered, Ramsay, Rillah, and Ralph the red-nosed rat crawled back through the Roman-vaulted rat-hole...

...and romped rapturously among
the roses, beside the rippling river,
under the radiant rainbow.